NICHOLAS CRICKET

By

Joyce Maxner

Illustrated by

William Joyce

Harper & Row, Publishers

LIBRARY OF CONGRESS CATALOGING-IN-PUBLICATION DATA

Nicholas Cricket
Text copyright © 1989 by Joyce Maxner
Illustrations copyright © 1989 by William Joyce
Printed in the U.S.A. All rights reserved.

Maxner, Joyce.
   Nicholas Cricket/words by Joyce Maxner; pictures by William
Joyce.
      p.   cm.
   Summary: Nicholas Cricket and the other members of the Bug-a-Wug
Cricket Band lead all the forest creatures in a musical celebration
of the night.
   ISBN 0-06-024216-7: $.—ISBN 0-06-024222-1 (lib. bdg.): $
   [1. Crickets—Fiction.   2. Bands (Music)—Fiction.   3. Animals—
Fiction.   4. Stories in rhyme.]   I. Joyce, William, ill.
II. Title.
PZ8.3.M44935Ni 1989   88-33076
[E]—dc19   CIP
                                                                    AC

1   2   3   4   5   6   7   8   9   10
First Edition

Nicholas Cricket plays every night
in the Bug-a-Wug Cricket Band.

Moonlight glows and summer wind blows,
rabbits come dancing on tip-tippy toes.
The music is just so grand!

Nicholas Cricket plays with all his might
in the Bug-a-Wug Cricket Band.

Little Lake shines and Little Stream winds,
peep-peep-peepers come dancing through the vines.
The music is just so grand!

Nicholas Cricket is a banjo picker
in the Bug-a-Wug Cricket Band.

Crickets play fiddles and guitars with middles
curvy and round as a rantum riddle
and ducks come dancing
ducky-hey-ducky-diddle.
The music is just so grand!

In the blue blue night
when the moon is bright
underneath the leaves of summer,
if we're quiet and quick
we can find Cricket Nick
and the washboard strummers
and the slap-a-spoon drummers
and the crick-crick-crickety kazoo hummers.

We can dance all night
'til the rosy dawn comes.
The music is just so grand!

Ladybugs strut and toads sashay,
moths and mantises wing their way,
snap-turtles swing and grasshoppers sway
while Nick and the crickets
just
    play
        and
           play.

The music is just so grand!

Then all the Bug-a-Wugs grow sleepy and still
and go back with the moonlight under the hill.
Back to the trees the peepers pop,
back to the hollow the rabbits hop,
back to the willows the weary ducks waddle
and back to our beds our tired legs toddle
to dream as Little Stream
winds
      its way
            into tomorrow.

The music was just so grand!
The music was just so grand!
The music was
just
    so
       grand!